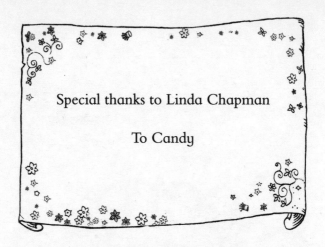

Special thanks to Linda Chapman

To Candy

ORCHARD BOOKS

First published in Great Britain in 2014 by Orchard Books
This edition published in 2016 by The Watts Publishing Group

5 7 9 10 8 6 4

A CIP catalogue record for this book is available from the British Library.

ISBN 978 1 40832 900 9

Printed in Great Britain by Clays Ltd, St Ives plc

Orchard Books
An imprint of Hachette Children's Group
Part of The Watts Publishing Group Limited
Carmelite House, 50 Victoria Embankment, London EC4Y 0DZ

An Hachette UK Company
www.hachette.co.uk
www.hachettechildrens.co.uk

Series created by Hothouse Fiction
www.hothousefiction.com

Puppy Fun

ROSIE BANKS

ORCHARD

This is the Secret Kingdom

Enchanted Palace

Contents

Good News

"It's almost half term!" Jasmine twirled around in the spring sunshine as she walked back from school with her best friends, Summer and Ellie. "Just a few more days. I can't wait!"

"It will be great to spend it together," said Ellie, her red curls bouncing on her shoulders as she skipped after Jasmine. "We can go swimming and play in the park and have sleepovers!"

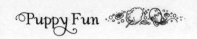

Jasmine's hazel eyes sparkled. "Do you think we'll also get to visit somewhere *else*?"

"I hope so!" said Ellie with a smile, knowing exactly what she meant. The three girls shared an amazing secret. They had a Magic Box that transported them to an enchanted land called the Secret Kingdom!

The Magic Box had been made by King Merry, the ruler of the magical land. He needed the girls' help to protect the kingdom from his mean sister, Queen Malice, who wanted to rule and make everyone as miserable as she was! The girls had helped the king many times now, and enjoyed lots of incredible adventures with the most amazing magical creatures.

Suddenly Ellie realised that Summer wasn't joining in the conversation. She looked round and saw their friend was biting her lip nervously as she hurried along the pavement.

Ellie frowned. "Are you okay, Summer?"

"I'm a bit worried about Rosa," Summer admitted. Her mum had taken their cat, Rosa, to the vet's that day because she hadn't been eating her food. "I know Mum said she would be fine but I can't help worrying."

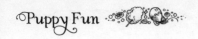

"We should head to your house straight away and find out what the news is," said Jasmine understandingly.

"Definitely," agreed Ellie.

"Thanks," Summer said gratefully, and the three friends ran all the way back to her house.

"How's Rosa?" The words tumbled out of Summer as soon as her mum opened the door.

"She's completely fine," Mrs Hammond said, smiling. "The vet checked her over and said there is absolutely nothing to worry about at all." Her smile broadened. "In fact, she's never been better!"

"That's brilliant!" Summer was so relieved Rosa was okay. "Where is she now?"

"She's upstairs on your bed." Summer's mum smiled.

The three girls ran upstairs. Rosa was curled up on Summer's duvet cover. She lifted her little black head as they came running in.

Summer stroked her and Rosa purred loudly. "I'm so glad you're all right," Summer said, kissing the top of Rosa's head.

"She looks happy to see you," said Jasmine, sitting down and stroking the cat's soft paws.

Listening to Rosa purring, Ellie grinned. "Hey, Summer. I know what

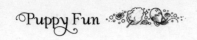

Rosa's favourite colour is — and it's the same as mine."

"What? Green?" asked Summer, puzzled.

Ellie grinned. "No, PURR-ple of course!"

Summer and Jasmine giggled. Ellie crouched down and tickled Rosa under the chin. "I'm glad you're all right, Rosa." As she petted the little cat, Ellie's knees bumped against something hard under the bed. "Is this the Magic Box?" Ellie said, pulling out a pink bag.

"Yes," said Summer. "I keep it in there so my brothers won't see it if they come into my room."

Ellie carefully took the Magic Box out of the pink bag. She stroked the wooden sides. They were carved with all sorts of magical creatures and studded with green gems. The lid of the box had a mirror on it and inside was a magic map of the Secret Kingdom that King Merry had given them and lots of other magical gifts, including a silver unicorn horn that let them talk to animals and an icy hourglass that could stop time!

"Oh, I do hope we get to go to the Secret Kingdom again soon," Ellie said longingly.

As she spoke, a flash of light ran across the mirrored lid. Rosa sat up on the bed with a surprised miaow. The box began to glow and a string of words swirled over the shining lid.

"There's a new message for us!" gasped Ellie.

Jasmine and Summer jumped off the bed and joined her on the floor. Even Rosa leaped down! The little cat sniffed at the sparkling box curiously while Ellie read out the words in the lid:

"Hello, dear friends, how do you do?
We are really missing you!
Look for turrets where rubies glow,
And come and see a magical show!"

As Ellie read out the last word, there was a bright flash of light and the box's lid opened. The magical map of the Secret Kingdom floated out and unfolded itself in front of their eyes. It wasn't like a normal map – all the pictures on it moved! There were mermaids swimming in the sea and unicorns cantering

through lush meadows, pixies skiing
down a mountain covered in pink snow
and golden flags flying from the pink
turrets of the Enchanted Palace.

Usually the girls had to work out
where in the kingdom the riddle wanted
them to go, but today there was only
one place it could be talking about! The
pink walls and turrets of King Merry's

Enchanted Palace were studded with glittering red rubies. The girls eagerly put their hands on the green gems of the box.

"Are you ready?" said Jasmine.

The others nodded. "King Merry's Enchanted Palace!" they all cried.

There was a tinkling of bells and another flash of light. The girls blinked. When they opened their eyes, a leaf was swooping around them. Sitting on top of it was a tiny pixie. She had a rose petal

hat perched on her blonde hair, and she wore a bright green-and-yellow top, a pink rose-petal skirt and curly-toed boots with a petal trim.

"Trixibelle!" cried the girls.

Trixi was a Royal Pixie. She helped look after King Merry, keeping the absent-minded king out of trouble. "Hello, girls!" she cried, flying round each of their heads. Rosa stretched and sat up with her ears pricked – she looked as if she thought Trixi might be fun to play with… Summer picked her up and gave her a cuddle, just in case she decided to try and catch the little pixie!

"It's lovely to see you again, girls," Trixi said, flying a loop-the-loop.

"It's great to see you too, Trixi!" said Jasmine eagerly.

"Is something the matter in the Secret Kingdom?" asked Summer. The girls were usually called to the Secret Kingdom to help out when there was trouble brewing there.

Trixi shook her head. "Don't worry. King Merry just wanted to send you a message because today is a very special day in the Secret Kingdom and he would love you to come and share it with us. Would you like to?"

"Yes, please!" the girls exclaimed.

"Then here we go!" Trixi tapped the ring she was wearing and called out in a silvery voice:

"Pixie magic in this ring,
Take us now to see the king!"

The girls were surrounded by a glowing cloud of green-and-gold sparkles. They gasped as the cloud whirled around them faster and faster, sweeping them off the ground. Summer suddenly realised something with a gasp – she was still holding Rosa! But it was too late to let go now. They were off on another Secret Kingdom adventure, and Rosa was coming too!

Keeper's Day

The girls twirled round and round
and then dropped towards the ground.
Jasmine felt something settle on top of
her dark hair and noticed that sparkling
tiaras sat on Summer and Ellie's heads
too. Their tiaras always appeared when
they arrived in the Secret Kingdom
and showed everyone in the land that
Jasmine, Summer and Ellie were Very
Important Friends of King Merry's!

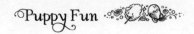

THUMP! Their feet hit the ground. Jasmine blinked her eyes open and saw that they were standing in the grand ballroom of King Merry's palace. An enormous glittering chandelier hung from the ceiling, made out of hundreds of real twinkling stars, and a grand staircase swept down into the room. A set of glass doors led out to the garden.

"We're in King Merry's palace again!"
Jasmine exclaimed, excitedly spinning
around in a circle.

"And Rosa's come with us!" cried
Summer, anxiously holding up the
surprised-looking cat. "I'm so sorry,
I forgot I was holding her!"

"Don't worry!" Trixi laughed. "She'll
be perfectly safe, and King Merry will be
delighted to meet her!"

Rosa didn't seem to have minded their
whirlwind trip at all – she was looking
around the room curiously.

"She's joining us for an adventure!"
Ellie laughed.

"Oh, castles and coronations, you've
arrived. Welcome, my friends –
welcome!"

The girls turned and saw King Merry

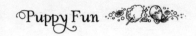

hurrying down the grand
staircase. He was wearing a
very smart red velvet cloak
that was embroidered
with pictures
of four animals:
a puppy, bird,
lion and seal.
His golden crown
was perched on
his white curls and
his bright eyes looked
at them from behind
his half-moon spectacles.

"King Merry!" cried Ellie, running over
and hugging him. He wasn't much taller
than she was – but he was so plump she
almost couldn't fit her arms around him!
"Thank you for inviting us here!"

King Merry looked delighted. "It's wonderful to see you again. I'm so glad you could be here for Keeper's Day!" He pushed his half-moon spectacles further up his nose.

"Keepers Day? What's that?" said Jasmine curiously.

But King Merry had been distracted by Rosa, who was still in Summer's arms. "Crowns and sceptres! A cat!" he cried.

"Yes, this is Rosa." Summer hoped the king wouldn't be cross. "I forgot to put her down when Trixi said her spell. I'll look after her and make sure she doesn't get in the way!"

But the kindly king was already hurrying over to Rosa. "Who's a beautiful little pussums then? Who's a pretty kitty cat?" He tickled Rosa under the chin. Rosa purred and rubbed her head against his hand. King Merry sighed fondly. "I'd love a pet cat but the trouble is they make me…make me… ATISHOO!"

He sneezed loudly and backed away. Trixi tapped her ring and a large red-and-white spotted handkerchief appeared in the king's hands. He blew his nose, making a sound like a trumpet. "Thank you, Trixi," he said gratefully.

"Cats make

the king sneeze if he gets too near,"
Trixi explained as the king blew his nose
again.

"Oh no! I'm really sorry," said
Summer. "I'll try to keep her close
to me."

"Don't be sorry at all, my dear," said
the king. "If I stay a little way off I'll
be fine, and it's lovely to meet Rosa. In
fact, today is all about having fun with
animals. Come and see!" He beckoned
them over to the glass doors that led to
the palace gardens and flung them open.

Immediately, the sound of laughter
and shouts of happiness flooded into
the room. The girls looked out into the
palace gardens. The flowerbeds were
filled with bright bell-shaped flowers that
played different musical notes as they

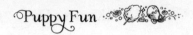

nodded in the gentle breeze, the trees were hung with striped candy canes and in the centre of the garden the lemonade fountain bubbled merrily, sending sweet bubbles up into the air. But it wasn't the fountain that caught the girls' attention – it was the enormous bouncy castle next to it. It looked just like the Enchanted Palace, with four pink turrets

studded with real rubies! Elves, pixies and
brownies were bouncing on it, laughing
and squealing.

"Oh, wow!" said Ellie. "There's a big
party going on!"

"It's lucky Queen Malice isn't here,"
said Jasmine as they walked through
the garden. "She'd hate to see everyone
having this much fun!"

Queen Malice was as horrible as King Merry was nice. She longed to rule the Secret Kingdom and was always coming up with evil schemes to try and take over from King Merry. Her last attempt had involved releasing six fairytale baddies into the kingdom. She'd hoped they would cause so much chaos and unhappiness that people would beg her to rule just to get rid of them! Luckily, King Merry had called Ellie, Jasmine and Summer and they had been able to put the baddies back in their book and restore peace to the land.

"What's happened to Queen Malice?" Summer asked the king. "When we were last here, she was stuck inside the fairytale book."

King Merry nodded. "She was,

but I decided to set her free after she apologised for causing so much trouble. Everyone deserves another chance, and I'd like to think my sister's changed her ways. She hasn't caused any trouble since then."

Ellie couldn't help thinking that the kindly king was wrong about his sister. Queen Malice was *really* mean. Ellie couldn't imagine that she had suddenly decided to change! "Maybe she's just taking her time to think up a really wicked plan," she said worriedly.

"Oh, dearie me," said the king, his glasses wobbling on his nose. "Don't go imagining things like that. I'm sure she's just at Thunder Castle, happily celebrating Keeper's Day like everyone here."

"So what *is* Keeper's Day?" asked Summer curiously.

"I shall tell you all about it, but before I start, let's get you all a special Keeper's Day drink." King Merry led the girls to four golden chairs in the beautiful rose garden. Lots of magical creatures came over to say hello to the girls as they walked through the gardens – there were unicorns, elves and tiny, sparkling fairies!

The king sat down in one of the chairs and settled his cloak around him. Trixi tapped the ring on her finger and magicked up three glasses of delicious fruit punch for the girls, and a bowl of cat treats for Rosa. The glasses were engraved with animals and there were slices of fruit cut in the shape of balloons, hearts, crowns and flowers floating in the

drinks. Rosa's bowl was decorated with
pictures of winged lions and tigers and
her biscuits were the shape of little fish!
The girls took a glass each and sat down.
Rosa sat by Summer's feet, purring
loudly.

"Keeper's Day happens once every hundred years in the Secret Kingdom," King Merry explained. "It is a time when the qualities of kindness, bravery, friendship and fun are renewed throughout the Secret Kingdom."

"How does it happen?" asked Jasmine curiously.

"On Keeper's Day, which is always the first day of Spring, the four Animal Keepers appear and travel around the Secret Kingdom for one week, spreading their special gifts of kindness, bravery, friendship and fun," the king replied, adjusting his glasses and sighing happily. "The Puppy Keeper brings the gift of fun, the Lion Keeper the gift of bravery, the Seal Keeper the gift of kindness and the Bird Keeper the gift of friendship.

Their magic is so powerful that it renews
and strengthens the feelings of kindness,
bravery, friendship and fun for the next
one hundred years! Everyone celebrates
Keeper's Day by having fantastic parties
and feasts."

Ellie sipped her drink. It was delicious
– like sweet strawberry lemonade that
fizzed on her tongue! "Where do the
Keepers come from?"

"Here!" Trixi flew over to a large
shield that was propped up on a golden
platform in the centre of the rose garden.
"This is normally kept in the throne
room, but on Keeper's Day it's brought
outside so that everyone can see the
Keepers for themselves!"

The shield was divided into four
sections and each section contained a

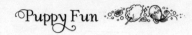

picture of a different animal. There was
a white puppy with lilac ears, a young
seal pup with creamy-white fur and a
pink heart-shaped patch on her chest,
a beautiful bird with glittery feathers in
different shades of blue and a golden lion

cub with a rainbow-coloured mane.

"But they're just pictures," said Summer.

"Aha, but they won't be when I have worked the magic," replied King Merry.

He reached into his pocket and pulled out a dusty old book.

"The Secret Spellbook!" cried Ellie, recognising it from one of their other adventures.

"Yes, it contains very powerful magic," said King Merry. "Which is exactly what I need today."

Jasmine exchanged excited looks with Ellie and Summer. What was going to happen? They hardly ever saw King Merry use magic!

King Merry cleared his throat and stepped onto the platform next to the

shield so that the gathered crowd could
see him. There was a buzz of excitement
as King Merry opened the book, sending
a cloud of glitter shooting up into the air!
The king began to read out a spell:

"With magic old and magic deep,
I call our Keepers from their sleep.
Travel east, west, south and north,
Animal Keepers – now spring forth!"

The king finished the
spell and shut the
book with a snap.
Suddenly a flash of
golden light shot
above their heads
and exploded into a
shower of bright sparks.

Summer, Ellie and Jasmine and the
gathered crowd gasped in amazement.
In the shield, the puppy gave a yap,
the bird stretched its wings, the lion cub
shook its mane and the seal flapped its
tail. Then, all at once, the four Animal
Keepers jumped out of the shield, grew to
Rosa's size and landed on the grass!

An Unwelcome Visitor

The girls and everyone in the rose
garden stared in delight at the four
Animal Keepers. The Seal Keeper opened
her mouth in a grin and clapped her
flippers together. The Puppy Keeper
gambolled around the girls' legs, his tail
wagging and his paws leaving a trail
of glittery lilac paw prints that faded
after a few moments. A young elf patted

the puppy on the head and was given
a big lick in return! The Bird Keeper
swooped around over their heads, blue
sparks flashing from her beautiful wings,
leaving glitter hanging in the air as she
flew. The watching fairies flew alongside
her – giggling happily as the bird's glitter
landed on their sparkling wings. The
Lion Keeper shook his rainbow-coloured
mane and gave a tiny roar of delight.

Rosa jumped down out of Summer's
arms. The lion cub pounced playfully
on Rosa's tail and soon
the pair of them
were rolling
around on the
floor together
like a couple
of kittens.

"Aren't they adorable?" said King Merry, chuckling in delight.

"Totally," said Ellie, bending down to stroke the seal pup who looked up at her with large melting eyes the colour of dark chocolate. She butted her head against Ellie's hand affectionately. Ellie noticed that she had a collar on with a golden heart-shaped charm hanging off it. Looking around, she saw that the other Keepers were wearing collars and charms too – the puppy's was shaped like a balloon, the bird's like a flower and the lion's like a crown.

Jasmine put out her
arm and the Bird
Keeper landed
on it. With
a squawk
she ruffled
her feathers,
making blue
glittery sparks
fly up around
Jasmine's head. As
they landed on her hair she felt them
tingle and tickle before they faded away.
Jasmine suddenly laughed out loud – she
felt so happy to be in the Secret Kingdom
with all her friends!

Summer crouched down and the puppy
licked her nose. "You're so cute!" she
giggled, giving him a hug. The puppy

rolled over onto his back and she tickled his pink tummy. His tail wagged.

"Oooh, I just want to bounce on the bouncy castle!" Summer cried. "It looks like such fun!"

Trixi smiled at the three friends. "The magic of the Animal Keepers is very powerful. Jasmine and Summer, the Bird Keeper and the Puppy Keeper are already making you feel full of friendship and fun! When the Keepers travel around the kingdom they strengthen and spread these feelings wherever they go."

"So what happens now?" Ellie asked King Merry.

"The four Animal Keepers will set off around the kingdom to spread their gifts of friendship, fun, bravery and kindness. The magic spell allows them all to fly and soar above the kingdom – and travel at great speeds! It will only take them a week to visit the whole kingdom. At the end of the week they'll return for a huge feast before they go back into the shield." King Merry clasped his hands together. "This truly is a day for happiness and laughter, joy and delight!"

Ellie had crouched down to pet the lion cub. "Look at his mane!" she exclaimed. "Isn't it amazing? It's changing colour!" As the girls watched, the lion suddenly stopped playing and stiffened, his mane flashing all the colours of the rainbow before turning a deep red.

Summer and Jasmine gasped in delight, but they quickly realised that King Merry and Trixi weren't joining in. They turned and saw the king and the pixie exchanging worried looks.

"What's the matter?" Jasmine asked.

King Merry pointed at the lion cub. "The Lion Keeper's mane only turns red when there is danger coming."

"The lion's gift is bravery," Trixi added. "He can always sense danger."

"But what danger could there be here?" said Summer, looking round. "Everything looks fine!"

Jasmine felt her stomach tighten. "Unless Queen Malice is here!"

"But she can't be," burst out King Merry. "She promised she wasn't going to be mean anymore—"

CRACK!

A flash of lightning lit up the garden and the sound of a cackling laugh rang through the air, interrupting King Merry.

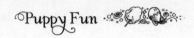

"It *is* Queen Malice!" cried Summer.

The Puppy Keeper and the Seal Keeper hid behind King Merry's legs while the Bird Keeper perched on his shoulder and hid her head under her wing. The Lion Keeper stood in front of the king and shook his red mane bravely. He roared but the sound was drowned out by Queen Malice's laughter.

"Where is she?" cried Ellie, looking round wildly as the laugh got louder and louder.

"Look, over there!" cried Jasmine, pointing at a fairground carousel a little way off. It had stopped spinning when the party goers had come over to see the Animal Keepers appear from the shield, but now it was slowly turning again. Summer and Ellie gasped as they saw that Queen Malice was on the carousel, riding on the back of a fierce-looking jet-black horse! With a click of her bony fingers, the horse leaped from the carousel and cantered towards them, almost knocking over a baby brownie who promptly burst into tears. The queen's eyes glittered like ice. In her hand was a long black wooden staff with

a thunderbolt on top.

The queen dismounted and the horse reared up, baring its teeth at King Merry as it galloped past, making the little king jump. Queen Malice laughed wickedly. "So, you thought I'd turned good, did you, brother?" she jeered, looking at King Merry. "Well, think again. I've come to stop your fun!"

Rosa arched her back and hissed at Queen

Malice. Summer hastily grabbed her. Who knew what the queen would do to the little cat if she got in her way!

"But today is Keeper's Day!" cried King Merry. "You can't cause trouble on Keeper's Day!"

"Ha!" taunted the queen. "This isn't just about your silly Keeper's Day party, dear brother, although seeing everyone having so much fun is *very* tiresome. I am fed up with the kingdom being full of kindness and bravery and all the other horribly happy feelings that those wretched animals spread around. Let's see what a lovely place the Secret Kingdom is when I lock the Animal Keepers up in the deepest dungeons of Thunder Castle – forever!"

Catch the Animal Keepers!

Just then, a big group of Queen Malice's horrid servants, the Storm Sprites, swooped down from the sky on their storm clouds, scooping up handfuls of dirt from the flowerbeds and throwing it at everyone. The baby unicorns reared up in fear as two of the nasty Storm Sprites chased the scared creatures away through the palace gardens.

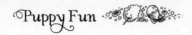

Queen Malice strode forward and reached out to the lion cub. The remaining Storm Sprites closed in on the Animal Keepers with their spindly fingers outstretched. The girls gathered closer to King Merry and the Keepers.

"Come with me, Animal Keepers,"
Queen Malice crowed. "I'm going to
lock you up! If you're not around to
spread your silly, happy feelings I'll soon
rule the kingdom – as everyone will be
too miserable and cowardly and mean
to stop me!"

"You're not taking the Animal
Keepers!" cried Jasmine, jumping in front
of the queen.

"And you'll *never* rule the kingdom,
we won't let you!" Ellie shouted.

"Go, Animal Keepers!" King Merry
shouted. "Once you're gone, she can't
catch you!"

There were four flashes of light – one
golden, one silver, one lilac and one blue
– and then all the animals disappeared!

"That's it! They've gone!" cried Trixi.

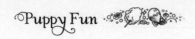

"They've already set off round the kingdom."

King Merry looked faint and mopped his forehead with his spotted handkerchief. "Thank goodness. Your plan has failed, sister!"

A cunning look flashed in the queen's eyes. "Really? Think again, brother. I still have a trick or two up my sleeve." She lifted her staff and the girls jumped back in alarm. What was she going to do now?

The queen gripped the staff:

"By mixing up this magic deep,
I shall make the kingdom weep.
Keepers' powers now reverse,
Change good to bad, they shall be cursed!"

There was a crash of
thunder. Four bolts
of green light
exploded out of
the top of her staff
and the Keepers'
golden charms
appeared, landing on
the grass in front of the girls.

Queen Malice shrieked in delight.
"Now see how much fun your precious
Keeper's Day is! Those foolish animals
may travel far and wide but they won't
bring goodness any more because I have
reversed their magic! The Puppy Keeper
will bring sadness and *no* fun. The Seal
Keeper will make people mean rather
than kind. The Bird Keeper will cause
people to be enemies, not friends, and the

Lion Keeper will make people cowardly rather than brave. By the time they have been all around the land, the Secret Kingdom will be a completely miserable place!" She cackled as she looked at the girls. "This is an even better plan then locking the animals away in my deepest dungeon! Now everyone will be so busy fighting with everyone else there will be no one to stop me and my Storm Sprites from taking over the kingdom!"

Queen Malice struck her staff against the ground and a flash of lightning surrounded her. She vanished, leaving only her triumphant laughter echoing around the grounds. Her Storm Sprites zoomed out of sight, giggling meanly.

Everyone stood in shocked silence as the queen's cackling faded. Jasmine was the first to speak. "We've got to do something to stop her!"

"But what?" said Trixi, her blue eyes brimming with tears. "The Animal Keepers are already travelling around the kingdom. Anyone who comes into contact with them will be affected by their mixed-up magic!"

"We need to catch them and try and reverse the queen's spell," said Ellie.

"But how can we do that?" asked Summer.

King Merry wrung his hands. "Oh, crowns and sceptres, this is terrible – simply terrible! I don't know how we can possibly get the Animal Keepers back. They normally travel around the kingdom for exactly one week and then return automatically to the shield. I don't

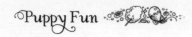

know how to find out where they are!"
Rosa started to struggle in Summer's
arms and Summer let her jump down.

The little cat trotted across the grass
to where the four golden charms lay

glinting in the sunlight. She batted at them with her paws.

Summer followed her and picked the charms up. "I wonder why the charms came back here?"

Trixi flew over. "It must be something to do with Queen Malice's spell."

"Well, the charms aren't much good without the Animal Keepers," said Jasmine. "We need to think about *where* we should start searching for them."

Summer clipped the charms onto Rosa's collar to keep them safe until they found the Animal Keepers. If *we find them*, she thought uneasily.

Ellie was staring at the shield. Now the animals had jumped out of it there were just the backgrounds of their pictures left – three of the squares had a misty, shimmering background, but where the puppy had been the background showed a square of coral pink with a large red stone at the top. She frowned. She was sure she'd seen that colour before, but where…?

"Of course!" she realised with a gasp. "I think that background shows one of the turrets of the palace," she told the others. "The red stone is one of the rubies!"

Summer's eyes widened. "Maybe it means the puppy is in the palace grounds somewhere!"

"But why would the puppy stay around here?" asked Jasmine with a frown.

Trixi thought for a moment. "Well, the Animal Keepers travel all around the kingdom, perhaps the puppy just wanted to explore the palace—"

Just then the girls heard a howl coming from somewhere nearby. It sent a shiver down their spines!

Searching High and Low

The howl faded away and the three girls looked at each other. "Do you think that was the Puppy Keeper?" whispered Summer.

"It definitely sounded like a dog," said Ellie.

"Let's start looking for the puppy over by the bouncy castle," said Jasmine, thinking fast. "Someone might have seen him go past."

"Great idea!" cried Trixi. She zoomed off in front of them, leading the way out of the rose garden, through the twisty magical maze and past the carousel.

The pink bouncy castle was straight in front of them. Summer noticed immediately that it was very quiet. The only sounds were sniffling and crying. "Oh dear," she said anxiously, looking at the others. "I think the Puppy Keeper might have come past here already."

They ran to the bouncy castle. All the elves, brownies and pixies were sitting on the edge, not bouncing at all. They looked very unhappy.

"Can you tell us what happened?" asked Trixi, flying over on her leaf.

"I don't know," sniffed an elf wearing a purple party dress. "We were all

having such a good time, then suddenly
it was as if a cold wind swept over us
and all we wanted to do was sit down
and cry."

The brownie next to her nodded. "I
don't want to jump and play any more."

"Me neither." A little pixie who was
hovering her leaf near the brownie's
shoulder gave a sob. "I just feel so…
so sad!" she wailed.

Ellie looked at the others. "The puppy has definitely passed by here! Now Queen Malice has cast her spell, he'll be making everything miserable instead of fun."

Summer felt so sorry for the sad party goers. She wished she could give them all a hug, but there were too many of them! "Don't worry, we'll sort this out," she promised them.

"Maybe we could all play some games?" Trixi suggested. "That might cheer everyone up."

Jasmine scanned the garden. "But we have to find the Puppy Keeper." She raised her voice and addressed everyone sitting on the bouncy castle. "Excuse me, has anyone seen a puppy?"

A small elf put up her hand. "I saw

one," she said sadly. "He was flying through the air and he went that way." She pointed towards the lemonade fountain.

The girls looked at the fountain. There, just above the tallest spout, was the faint outline of a set of sparkly paw prints in the air!

"Look!" said Jasmine. "He went that way!" She turned to the others. "Let's go after him."

"But we can't just leave everyone feeling so miserable," said Summer, her heart going out to the unhappy people in front of her.

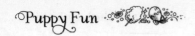

"We have to!" said Ellie.

"Or…" Summer thought of something. "You two could go and follow the footprints while Trixi and I try to cheer everyone up here."

Jasmine and Ellie nodded and set off.

"Maybe I could make some magic fireworks," Trixi suggested to Summer. "Everyone loves fireworks!" She tapped her ring and green-and-silver stars shot up into the sky and exploded in a shower of sparks. The elves, pixies and brownies looked up but just sighed.

"All those poor sparks, just vanishing into nothing!" said one brownie as the sparks blinked out.

"It's so sad when they fade away," said another.

"One bang and then they're gone forever," said another one dismally.

Everyone started to cry.

"Oh dear, that didn't work!" said Trixi in alarm.

Just then, King Merry ran over to join them. He was puffing, his cheeks pink from the exercise. Rosa was beside him. Seeing Summer, she gave a happy mew and trotted over, the charms on her collar making a tinkling sound as they jangled against one another. As she reached Summer, she pushed her head against Summer's leg and then rolled over in the sun, her front paws batting at the golden charms around her neck. She looked so cute that Summer, Trixi and King Merry all laughed.

All of a sudden, one of the charms started to glow. Summer frowned and reached for it. It was the puppy's balloon-shaped charm. "Look!" she gasped. "There are some words on this charm now."

She was right! Lines of faint words were shining out on the charm. Summer started to read them out:

*"To call me back from where I roam,
Use this spell to bring me home..."*

"Hmmm, it seems to be some sort of clue," she said. "But only some of it has appeared." Her mind raced. They needed to make more words appear on the charm, but how?

Just then, Ellie and Jasmine came running back. "We couldn't find the Puppy Keeper," said Jasmine. "Although we did see more glittery pawprints by the moat next to the giant goldfish, and in the flower beds…" She trailed off as she saw everyone staring at Rosa. "What's going on?"

Summer explained. "We were watching Rosa playing with the charms and then the puppy's charm started to glow—" She broke off with a gasp. "Of course! We were laughing! Maybe if we're all having fun, more words will appear!"

"Great idea!" said Jasmine. She

scrambled up onto the bouncy castle.
"I know what I find fun… Bouncing!"
She jumped up and down. "Join in,
Ellie!"

Ellie flung herself onto the bouncy
castle. It was like trying to walk on
massive wobbly pillows! Summer scooped
Rosa up and watched as Ellie tumbled
over, laughing. Summer glanced at the
charm on Rosa's collar. "It's starting
to shine again but no more words have
appeared!" she called.

Jasmine jumped even higher. "Come
on, King Merry! You join in, too!"

She and Ellie helped the king heave
himself onto the castle. He bounced
around, his crown and glasses
wobbling as he held hands with them.
"Oh goodness gracious! Oh my!

This is…this is…such FUN!"

Trixi swooped around his head.
"Higher, Your Majesty! Higher!" she
giggled.

The watching brownies and elves

started to smile as they watched the king jump higher and higher, his cloak flying up into the air. "Whoopee!" he cried.

The brownies and elves began to climb back on to the bouncy castle. They helped each other up and started to join in with the king.

"This is fun!" cried one, laughing.

"It's working!" cried Summer, seeing the charm glowing brighter and brighter. More words were appearing now, but as she bent down to read them a dark shadow fell across her. She looked up and saw two figures flapping down towards the bouncy castle. They had large grey wings, mean pointed faces and outstretched bony fingers. Summer's stomach flipped over. The Storm Sprites were back!

"Go away!" she shouted at them.

"NO!" they shrieked. "We're going to pop that stupid pink bouncy castle and stop all this fun!"

Trixi's Brilliant Spell

There was nothing Summer could do. She shouted and yelled but the Storm Sprites swooped down and jabbed at the bouncy castle walls with their long sharp nails.

Jasmine and Ellie bounced over to see what was happening. The air was already rushing out of the castle.

"Everyone out!" yelled Jasmine as the castle started to collapse.

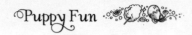

The sprites screamed with glee as the brownies, pixies and elves came tumbling out. King Merry bounced out and landed on one of the mats on his bottom. His crown had been knocked to one side and his white curls were standing up wildly around his head.

The sprites flew round, cackling, as the castle lost all its air and sank down until it was just a mound of floppy pink plastic on the ground. The brownies, pixies and elves sat down on top of it and started to cry again.

"You horrible things!" Jasmine shouted at the Storm Sprites.

"Tee hee!" they jeered. "You're going to be so busy fixing the things that we mess up that you'll never find that silly puppy and Queen Malice will take over the kingdom!"

"We can't let them beat us," Summer said to Ellie and Jasmine. "We have to find the puppy before he leaves the palace and makes people in other parts of the kingdom unhappy, too. There has to be something else that we can do."

Ellie turned to Trixi who was hovering close by on her leaf. "Can you do anything with your magic, Trixi?" she said in a low voice so the sprites couldn't hear. "Something that will let everyone have fun without the Storm Sprites interfering?"

Trixi considered it. "I could do something inside the palace – we could shut the doors to keep the sprites out so they couldn't spoil it. Then everyone can enjoy themselves and we can have enough fun to work out the rest of the riddle."

"Oh yes!" gasped Summer.

"Oh please, Trixi!" whispered
Jasmine. "I'm sure you can do something
brilliant."

Trixi thought for a moment then
tapped her ring and called out a spell:

"To the palace bring lots of fun,
Games and treats for everyone!"

Gold light exploded through the palace,
shining out through the windows and
doors. Fairground music flooded out
and the air was filled with the smell of
delicious cakes and candyfloss.

King Merry ran to the ballroom doors.
"Oh my goodness gracious! Trixi, you
wonderful, amazing pixie! Everyone,
come and see what Trixi has done!"

The brownies and elves sighed glumly

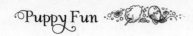

but obediently trooped into the palace.
The girls hurried after them, shutting and
locking the doors firmly behind them so
the mean Storm Sprites couldn't follow
them.

"Oh, Trixi! This is amazing!"
exclaimed Ellie. The ballroom was
completely transformed! It was now filled
with giant pink-and-purple balloons that
bobbed through the air with long strings
attached. A twisty rainbow-coloured

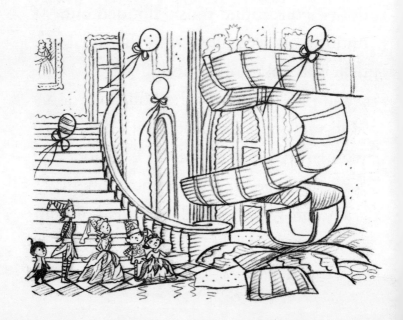

slide filled the centre of the room, ending in a massive pile of bouncy cushions.

A huge silver tree grew up out of the floor. Its glittering branches were hung with big round balls of pink candyfloss and red toffee apples.

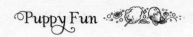

"Oh, wow!" breathed Summer.

"Look in the other rooms!" grinned Trixi, turning a loop-the-loop.

The girls and the king ran into the great entrance hall of the palace, Rosa ran along beside Summer, her tail waving happily in the air. All the staircases had been turned into slides and the walls were hung with rainbow ribbons and sparkling twinkle-twinkle bunting that glittered and shone. Against one wall a long table was filled with huge crystal bowls of ice cream, and above them hovered shakers filled with silver, chocolate and rainbow-coloured sprinkles!

The next room was filled with huge bubbles. "Bouncing bubbles," Trixi explained. "You can jump inside them and enjoy a bubble ride around the palace!"

"This is perfect, Trixi!" said Jasmine happily. "Everyone will soon be having so much fun that the rest of the words will appear on the charm in no time!"

"I'm not so sure," said King Merry anxiously. "Look at everyone's faces."

Summer, Jasmine and Trixi looked round. Despite all the amazing things around them, the elves, pixies and brownies were still looking miserable. A few of them were helping themselves to ice cream cones, but they each sat down on their own and licked them sadly. Another climbed up the staircase-

slide but even whizzing down it didn't
seem to make him happy. The rest
simply sat down and sighed. A feeling of
gloom hung over everyone. Summer felt
her own spirits sinking. *Maybe there's
nothing we can do*, she thought sadly,
picking up Rosa and hugging her.

"It's hopeless," sighed Ellie, sitting
down. "We're never going to be able to
make people happy."

Trixi flopped on her leaf. "I should
never even have tried."

"Yes, I might as well accept that the
Secret Kingdom is ruined," sighed King
Merry. His lower lip wobbled.

Rosa purred and nuzzled Summer's
cheek, tickling her with her whiskers.
Summer smiled despite the feeling of
sadness pressing down on her.

"King Merry's right," said Jasmine, nodding glumly. "It looks like Queen Malice has really won this time."

Summer blinked as she heard the words. It was so unlike Jasmine to say something like that. She realised that the puppy's magic had started affecting them too! *That means he must be somewhere close by…* Just then, something caught her eye. She looked up, and there, sitting on one of the bouncing bubbles, was the Puppy Keeper!

"Look, there he is!" she cried, jumping up and pointing to where the puppy had been. But when she looked back, he was gone! Putting Rosa on the ground, Summer jumped inside one of Trixi's magical bubbles and bounced her way up to the ceiling to see if she could

spot the Animal
Keeper, but he
was nowhere
to be seen.

Bouncing
her way back
down, Summer
looked around
at her glum
friends. She realised
that getting up and doing something had
made her feel so much better! "We can't
think this way," she said. Rosa purred
loudly in agreement. "We're only feeling
like this because the Puppy Keeper is
close by and his mixed-up magic is
affecting us. It's hard to catch the puppy
because he's so small and fast, but if we
carry on helping everyone cheer up,

hopefully more words will appear on the charm and I'm sure the words will help us find the puppy!"

She glanced around the room and realised something. "Maybe the problem is that everyone's just doing things on their own. No one's talking to each other or playing together."

Ellie nodded and looked round. "You're right. We know it's always much more fun when we share things."

"So, let's get everyone doing stuff together!" said Summer.

Jasmine lifted her chin. "Yes. We can't give in to feeling miserable. We've got to fight it and help everyone else fight it too! We should work together to make everyone cheery again. Then we can read the words on the charm

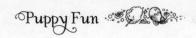

and get the puppy!"

"Come on! Let's get everyone playing!" cried Ellie.

At that moment, two Storm Sprites came swooping down from upstairs. "You thought you could keep us out!" taunted one. "But we got in through the king's bedroom window!"

"You're as silly as stink toads," cackled the other.

Ellie ignored the horrible creatures. They weren't going to spoil Summer's plan!

Taking no notice of the jeering sprites, she ran over to a group of elves sitting on the floor and started to organise a game of musical bumps. "Jump up everyone!" she urged. "This is a game from my world. I'll ask some of the brownies with instruments to play a tune and then you're going to jump up and down until the music stops. Then you have to sit down as fast as you can. It'll be fun!"

Summer went to the ice cream table with Rosa. "Come on!" she said to the nearby pixies. "Let's make up a funny story while we eat our ice cream." She started handing out the tiny cones. "It can be about a naughty kitten. Rosa was always getting into trouble when she was little so I've got lots of ideas!"

"And who wants to dance with me?" cried Jasmine, grabbing the brownies' hands. Trixi tapped her ring and magicked up some more instruments. Jasmine handed them out to a few of the brownies and encouraged them to start playing. Then she started to dance.

At first the brownies didn't really want
to, but soon they were smiling and
dancing an energetic polka while Jasmine
skipped around and urged them on, her
dark hair flying. Two unicorns joined
in the jig, tapping a merry rhythm with
their shiny silver hooves.

King Merry joined in. "Over here for
the helter skelter!"

Trixi urged some of the elves and
brownies who weren't doing anything
to follow the king and Ellie joined them
too. "Let's all go down together!" she
cried as she climbed the steps.

"Geronimo!" cried King Merry,
shooting down the slide first, his feet in
the air and his hands waving wildly.
The rest of them followed in a long line.
They whizzed faster and faster until they

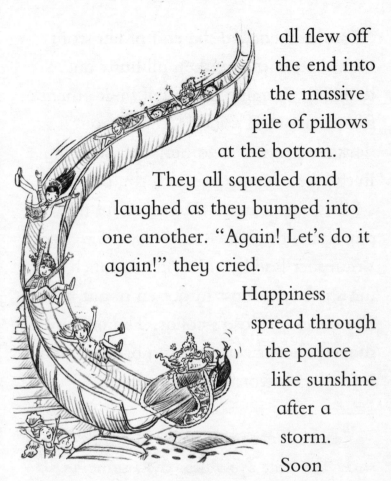

all flew off
the end into
the massive
pile of pillows
at the bottom.
They all squealed and
laughed as they bumped into
one another. "Again! Let's do it
again!" they cried.

Happiness
spread through
the palace
like sunshine
after a
storm.
Soon
everyone was laughing, helping one
another to candyfloss and ice cream and
making up new games of their own.

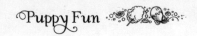

Summer reached the end of her story with the pixies and they all burst out laughing, running off to tell their other friends about it.

Jasmine ran over to her. "It's working! Everyone's happy again."

Ellie joined them. "What about the puppy's charm?"

Summer had been having so much fun she had almost forgotten about it! She checked Rosa's collar. The balloon-shaped charm was glowing brightly and a few more words had appeared:

"To call me back from where I roam,
Use this spell to bring me home.
Say my name and spin around..."

but the rhyme was still incomplete.

Just then there were more shrieks of
laughter from up above them. The two
Storm Sprites had been caught up in
the fun too! They were riding in two
of the giant bubbles and bumping into
each other happily, their wings flapping.

They laughed and chortled and Summer
couldn't help giggling at the sight of
them. Suddenly there was a bright flash.
Summer realised that all the words had
appeared!

"We've done it!" she cried. "We can
read what the charm says!"

The Charm's Magic

The words shone on the golden charm, casting a shimmering light on the rest of Rosa's collar. The girls gathered round and read it.

"It's a spell to get the puppy back!" Jasmine said excitedly.

"Let's say it together and see what happens," said Ellie. The girls gathered around Rosa and read out the words together:

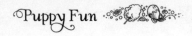

"To call me back from where I roam
Use this spell to bring me home.
Say my name and spin around,
Then tap your heels upon the ground!"

The girls smiled at each other and
called out "Puppy Keeper!" all together.
Then they linked arms and spun around,
before finally tapping their heels on the
ground.

There was a flash of golden light and suddenly the puppy came sliding down one of the slides! He landed in the cushions and flopped his head down on his paws, looking very unhappy.

A feeling of gloom was already spreading through the room again.

"He's making everyone feel sad again," said Jasmine in alarm. "We've got to break Queen Malice's curse!"

"But how?" said Trixi as one by one the elves and brownies nearby stopped playing and sat down on the floor, looking miserable.

Something was tugging at Summer's memory. She remembered how all four charms had appeared out of nowhere when the wicked queen had cast her spell. There must be some link between the spell and the charm. But what? *Think*, she told herself.

Rosa jumped down out of Summer's arms and went over to the sad puppy. The charms clinked on her collar and he pricked his ears and looked up. He stared at the charm on the cat's collar and then started to whine.

"He wants his collar charm back!" Summer gasped. "Maybe giving him back his charm will break the curse?"

She ran to Rosa and gently took the charm off her collar. The Puppy Keeper ran over to her and put his paws on her knees. He gave a small hopeful yap.

"Here you are," Summer whispered, clipping the charm onto his collar.

CRASH!

There was a sudden clap of thunder.

The puppy jumped in the air and then raced around the room barking happily, leaving trails of lilac paw prints wherever he went. Summer felt happiness whoosh through her like fizzy lemonade, rushing from her toes to her head. She started to laugh and realised everyone else was laughing too. The gloom and unhappiness had completely gone! Rosa chased after the puppy and they rolled around together on the floor, the golden charm glinting in the light. Everyone whooped and cheered.

"My sister's spell has been broken!" cried King Merry.

The Puppy Keeper raced over to the king and bounced around, his tail wagging. King Merry bent down and the puppy covered his face with excited licks. King Merry chuckled. "Go, my furry friend. Travel around the kingdom, bring fun instead of misery, laughter instead of tears!"

The puppy yapped, licked each of the girls goodbye and then jumped into the air and disappeared in a flash of lilac light.

Jasmine hugged Summer. "That was a brilliant idea!"

Ellie joined in. "You saved the day."

"We saved it together!" said Summer happily. Rosa trotted over and Summer scooped her up. The remaining three charms on the cat's collar glinted.

"What about the other Animal Keepers?" Ellie said. "Will the spell have broken for them too?"

King Merry shook his head. "No, I think they will still be under my sister's curse until their charms are returned to them."

"We have to find them then!" said Ellie. "And the sooner the better."

"King Merry and I will keep a close eye on the kingdom to see if we can work out where the other Keepers have gone," Trixi said. "They only have one week to travel around the whole kingdom, so hopefully we'll find the next one very soon. As soon as we spot anything we'll send a message to you. But for now, you'd better be getting home."

"We'll check the Magic Box every day," promised Jasmine. "As soon as it glows, we'll come back to help."

Ellie nodded firmly. "Queen Malice won't get away with this."

"Thank you, my dears," said King Merry gratefully. "I don't know what we would do without you."

Summer hugged Rosa. "Should I give you the three other charms back, King Merry?"

"No, you keep them for now," said the king, tickling Rosa under her chin and then sneezing loudly. "I'm sure Rosa will be an excellent guardian. Goodbye, girls!"

Trixi flew around them as they all called out goodbye and then she tapped her ring. The next second, the girls were whisked away in a sparkling cloud.

With a faint tinkle of bells they arrived back in Summer's bedroom. Rosa gave a surprised miaow. Summer looked around – no time ever passed when they were away in the Secret Kingdom, so no one would ever know that they'd gone. She let Rosa go and the little cat jumped onto her bed.

"I can't believe we've started another adventure," said Ellie.

"Another very exciting adventure!" said Jasmine, her eyes sparkling.

"Look!" said Summer suddenly. The Magic Box was on the floor beside them, but it was open and the map was lying on the floor. Something about the map had changed. Summer looked more closely and saw that there was now a picture of the Keeper's shield in one corner. There was a silhouette of the Puppy Keeper in one corner, but the other three pictures were empty, with pale, shimmering backgrounds. "The shield is on the map too," she said, pointing it out to the others.

Ellie frowned. "Isn't it odd how we saw a background for the puppy on the shield but the background, of the other animals were really hazy, just like they are on

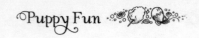

this picture. I wonder why?"

Summer and Jasmine thought about it.

"Well... I suppose it could be because the puppy had stopped at the palace," said Summer, thinking out loud. "Maybe when the other animals stop their backgrounds will become clear too?"

"I hope so," said Jasmine. "If we're going to track them down and give them back their charms, we're going to need all the clues we can get!"

The map folded itself up and flew back into the box as if to say that the girls had worked out what they needed to know. The lid shut with a snap. For a moment the lid glowed and then the light faded.

"Oh, I *do* hope we can reunite the other Keepers with their charms soon," said Summer.

"We will," Jasmine told her. "We won't let Queen Malice ruin the Secret Kingdom."

Ellie looked at Rosa who was curled up on the bed. "No way. We'll make the Secret Kingdom absolutely PURR-fect again!"

Summer and Jasmine giggled, and Ellie linked arms with them both. "You know, I have a feeling that this is going to be the most exciting half-term holiday ever!" she said with a grin.

In the next Secret Kingdom adventure, Ellie, Summer and Jasmine must find the

Magic Seal

Read on for a sneak peek...

No More School!

"Hold on tight!" called Summer as she pushed Ellie and Jasmine on the roundabout at Honeyvale Park.

"Faster!" gasped Jasmine.

Summer gave the roundabout one last big push and jumped on too. Jasmine whooped as they all spun round.

Looking up at the blue sky Summer

laughed, feeling as though they would keep spinning round for ever, but gradually the roundabout got slower and finally stopped completely.

Jasmine jumped off. "I love roundabouts!"

"Me too," Ellie said happily.

"Do you know what they remind me of?" Summer asked.

"I bet I do!" Ellie checked around, but there was no one close enough to hear. "Whizzing off to the Secret Kingdom?" she whispered.

Summer nodded. "Yes!" The three friends often visited a magic land called the Secret Kingdom. It was ruled by a jolly king called King Merry, and lots of amazing magical creatures such as elves and unicorns lived there. Whenever they went to the Secret Kingdom, King Merry's Royal Pixie, Trixi, whisked the girls away in a sparkling cloud that spun them round and round – just like the roundabout, but a hundred times better!

"I hope we get another message from the Secret Kingdom soon," said Jasmine. "Half term would be the perfect time to have some more adventures as we'll be spending lots of time together."

Ellie's green eyes sparkled. "You're right, although any time's the perfect time to have an adventure!"

"I think we should go back to my house and check the Magic Box," said Summer. "Another message might be waiting for us."

King Merry had invented a magical box that sent the girls a riddle whenever they were needed in the kingdom. The girls were often called to the kingdom because the king's wicked sister, Queen Malice, was desperate to rule the Secret Kingdom. She was determined to cause trouble until the kingdom was hers!

The girls ran to pick up their school bags and then set off for Summer's house.

"No more school for a week," said Jasmine, practising a pirouette as they walked.

Ellie grinned. "I bet I know what the elves learn at their school in the Secret Kingdom."

"What?" Summer asked.

"The *elf*-abet of course!" Ellie said.

Summer and Jasmine both groaned. Ellie giggled. "Come on!" she said, breaking into a run. "Race you back!"

Mrs Hammond, Summer's mum, opened the front door. "Hi, girls! How was your last day at school? There's lemonade in the fridge and I've made some fresh popcorn for you."

"Thanks, Mum," said Summer. "Can we take it upstairs?"

"Sure," her mum replied.

Summer, Ellie and Jasmine carried drinks and the bowl of popcorn upstairs. The window was open and they could hear Summer's younger brothers playing outside in the garden. Summer's room was covered with posters of animals. There were lots of books stacked up on two shelves and a white fluffy rug on the floor. A little black cat was curled up on her bed.

Summer ran over and gave the cat a

kiss. "Hi, Rosa!"

Rosa purred and Summer stroked her soft coat. "I'm surprised you're not outside in the garden. You seem to like my bed a lot at the moment."

Rosa rubbed her head against Summer's hand. Three charms jingled together on her collar.

Jasmine gently touched the shimmering charms. One was shaped like a heart, one like a flower and the last was shaped like a crown.

"The Animal Keepers' magic charms," she said softly. "We must get them back to the three missing Keepers before any more damage is done in the Secret Kingdom."

The three girls looked serious for a moment as they all remembered what had happened in the Secret Kingdom the last time they had been there.

Once every hundred years, kind King Merry used the Secret Spellbook to summon four Animal Keepers from a magical shield. The Keepers were a puppy, a seal, a bird and a lion cub and their job was to magically travel all around the Secret Kingdom, spreading fun, kindness, friendship and courage as they went.

Read
Magic Seal
to find out what happens next!

Secret Kingdom

Have you read all the books in Series Four?

Meet the magical Animal Keepers of the Secret Kingdom, who spread fun, friendship, kindness and bravery throughout the land!

Be in on the secret... Discover the first enchanting series!

Series 1

When Jasmine, Summer and Ellie discover the magical land of the Secret Kingdom, a whole world of adventure awaits!

Secret Kingdom

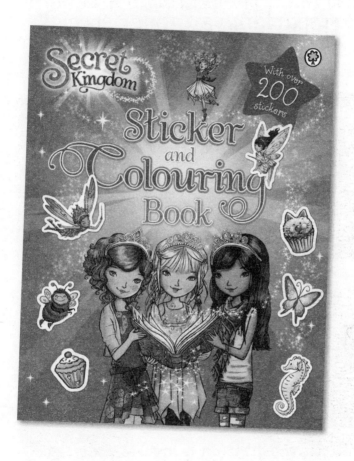

The magical world of Secret Kingdom comes to life with this gorgeous sticker and colouring book. Out now!

Look out for the next sparkling summer special!

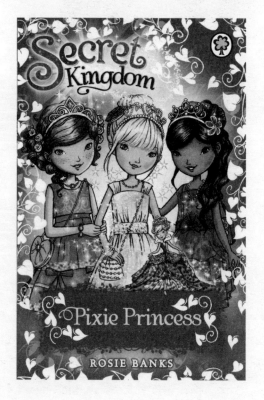

Join the girls on a special pixie-sized adventure!

Available
June 2014

Secret Kingdom

Don't miss the next amazing series!

It's Ellie, Summer and Jasmine's most
important adventure yet... Queen Malice has
taken over the Secret Kingdom! The girls must
find four magic jewels to make King Merry
a new crown and return him to the throne –
but where in the kingdom can the gems be?

Available
August 2014

Secret Kingdom Shield Competition!

Can you help best friends
Ellie, Summer and Jasmine solve the riddles?

At the back of each Secret Kingdom adventure in this set (books 19-22) is a different riddle for you to solve. The answers are all connected to a character featured in this set of Secret Kingdom books.

Here's how you enter the competition:

✳ Read and solve the riddle on the page opposite

✳ Once you think you know the answer, go to
www.secretkingdombooks.com
to print out the special shield activity sheet

✳ Draw the animal that you think is the answer
to the riddle on the shield

✳ Once you've drawn all four correct answers,
send your entry into us!

The lucky winners will receive a bumper Secret Kingdom goody bag full of treats and activities.

Please send entries to:
Secret Kingdom Shield Competition
Orchard Books, 338 Euston Road, London, NW1 3BH

Don't forget to add your name and address.

Good luck!

Closing date: 31st October 2014

Riddle one

With a waggy
tail and
sparkling eyes,
Can you guess
this Keeper to
win a prize?

The answer is

....

Secret Kingdom

A magical world of
friendship and fun!

Join the Secret Kingdom Club at

www.secretkingdombooks.com

and enjoy games, sneak peeks and lots more!

You'll find great activities, competitions, stories
and games, plus a special newsletter for
Secret Kingdom friends!